Pipi and Pou Review

It's [the] wry humour from the characters that makes this book so entertaining. Pipi and Pou are well-rounded characters who, despite their superhero abilities, still feel like real kids with their own problems and priorities: 'They loved being superheroes. It was just that sometimes they wanted to relax, to be lazy, to read a book, play on screens, watch television,' Tipene writes. The depth of the characters made these books spring to life from the page.

Pipi and Pou show us that we don't need supernatural abilities to be kaitiaki for the environment, and that protecting the natural world is rewarding, community-building, and fun. These books are sure to be a hit with kids and adults alike. I'm looking forward to seeing what more adventures this trio of kaitiaki get up to.

- **Hannah Marshall** *(The Sapling)*

Recipient of a 2022 Contestable Fund Grant from Copyright Licensing New Zealand

Produced with the support of: ARTS COUNCIL OF NEW ZEALAND TOI AOTEAROA

First published by OneTree House Ltd, New Zealand, 2023

Text © Tim Tipene, 2023
Illustrations © Isobel Te Aho-White, 2023

9781990035289

All rights reserved. No part of this publication may be reproduced, stored in a retrieval system or transmitted in any form or by any means, electronic, mechanical, photocopying, recording or otherwise, without the prior permission of the publisher.

Printed in New Zealand, YourBooks

10 9 8 7 6 5 4 3 2 1   3 4 5 6 7 / 2

Pipi and Pou
and the
TENTACLES OF THE DEEP

Tim Tipene

illustrated by
Isobel Te Aho-White

KAITIAKI

Guardians and Protectors of the natural world.

NANA

A kuia and a tohunga, an expert in the natural world, who holds experience and wisdom.

She leads and guides her mokopuna, Pipi and Pou, through their adventures in being kaitiaki.

Nana is also a master chef.

PIPI

When she runs, she flies.
She likes to win and
she loves to sing.
With the words, 'Pouākai,
haere mai!', Pipi transforms
into a Pouākai, a giant eagle.
Along with her cousin, Pou, Pipi
assists her grandmother, Nana, in
caring for and protecting the natural
world.

POU

A keen rugby player who also loves
being in water and coming first
against his cousin.
He is mighty. He is fierce.
When Pou cries, 'Taniwha, kia kaha!',
he changes into a Taniwha.
Like Pipi and Nana, Pou is a
superhero for the environment.

Tahi

Nana's old car coughed and spluttered, blowing bubbles of waiata and aroha from the exhaust, as it pulled up at a beach, under a row of Christmas coloured pōhutukawa. Nana's waka, Betsy, didn't run on petrol or power. It ran on songs and love.

'Here we are,' the tohunga smiled beneath her sunglasses.

Pipi was sitting next to her in the front passenger seat.

'Good thing you found a park,' she said, gesturing at all the other vehicles lining the side of the road.

Nana's hands rested on the steering wheel. She eyed the golden sand, the blue sea, and the white foam-crested waves rolling into shore.

'Ātaahua, what a beautiful day,' she uttered, momentarily lost in the bliss of her surroundings. She turned to her moko. 'Make sure you two have got plenty of sunscreen on. It's gonna be a hot one.'

'Already done, Nan,' Pipi replied, showing the residue of grease on her hands leftover from applying the cream.

Pou pulled the latch and pushed the back door open with his foot. His eyes scanned the many people dotted in groups along the shore.

'They're here,' he announced, spotting members of their whānau together on the beach. The relatives were gathered on and around woven flax mats which had been spread out on the sand.

Pipi climbed out of the car. 'Cool, Uncle Hēmi brought his guitar.'

'You can show him how to play it, girl,' Nana chuckled, standing on the grass and donning her apricot-coloured, straw sun hat which was adorned with flowers.

Nana and her moko took bags and kai from the back of the waka and carried them down onto the beach to join their whanaunga.

'Kia ora, Nan!' everyone sang when she neared.

'Tēnā koutou,' Nana beamed. The

grandmother loved nothing better than to be with family and to see all her other mokopuna. She gave everyone a hongi, a kiss on the cheek, and a hug.

Pipi and Pou did the same. Then they ran to the water with their cousins.

Nana leaned on her tokotoko, watching the waves and smelling the sea breeze.

'Ahh, this is the life,' she breathed.

'You can relax now, Nan,' said Aunty Kaia, who was standing nearby tying up a little girl's hair.

'Āe,' Nana nodded. She sat down on one of the woven mats and watched Pipi and Pou play with their relatives in the shallows. Tamanuiterā, the sun, was shining bright and there wasn't a cloud in the sky. It was a perfect day for the beach, yet as much as she tried, Nana couldn't relax. She turned to see an old man standing on the grass under a bright red and green pōhutukawa. He was watching her. Nana had first noticed the elder hanging around when she had been unpacking her car.

'Kei te pēhea koe, Nan?' Aunty Kaia asked, sitting down and taking hold of her hand. 'How have you been?'

The tohunga smiled at the middle-aged woman.

'Kei te pai, dear,' she answered. 'You know me. I like to keep busy.'

'Still driving all over the motu I hear?' muttered Aunty Kaia, shaking her head. 'Forever trying to better the world, eh? We would be lost without you.'

Nana was renowned for attending different hui at marae up and down the country, and for supporting and offering āwhina to her people.

'It's not just me,' stated Nana. 'I'm slack compared to other kuia. Do you know that I missed two meetings last week because I was busy doing other things?'

'Really?' said Aunty Kaia, raising her brow and knowing full well that the old woman was never one to accept any praise or recognition.

Nana looked back at the grass, but only saw a flock of tarāpunga, red-billed seagulls, squabbling over bits of discarded food. She noticed that the old man had gone.

Rua

After Pipi and Pou had had a big play with their cousins in the surf they returned to the rest of the whānau on the beach for a feed. A feast had been laid out in the middle of the mats. There were all sorts of food; freshly made rēwena bread, mussel chowder, chop suey, raw fish in coconut cream, chicken with Nana's secret-ingredient stuffing, and Aunty Kaia's weight-reducing, multi-coloured salad. There was even fresh kina, which Pipi loves but Pou can't stand.

The children's mouths were watering as they waited for someone to lead the karakia mō te kai. No one could eat until thanks for the food had been said.

Sitting on the edge of the woven mats, Nana was instructing her smaller moko to bring her sea shells. She was especially keen on the cone type that had once been home to sea snails but which were now empty. Nana had swapped her sunglasses for her specs and was examining each shell, searching for a small hole near the peak of the cone.

'Aha,' she muttered, showing the mark to the little ones. 'Titiro, look see, this one was also punctured by te wheke. The octopus has all sorts of tools in its mouth, a beak, a barbed tongue, and even a tooth for drilling into shells like these. They love eating sea snails.'

Nana put each cone shell to her ear and listened to it.

'Kāo, not that one,' she said, placing that shell back on the pile. 'Find me another.'

A little boy found a large, white cone with pink speckles that was partly buried in the sand. Unbeknown to him it was an opal top shell, a matangongore. Using his fingers, he dug it out.

'That one,' Nana asserted when she saw what he had found. 'Bring it here, my darling.'

The boy carried the cone over in two hands like it was some precious treasure, and gave it to Nana. The other small moko circled around the tohunga to watch. Nana gently tapped the shell against her hand, shaking out the sand from inside, and brushed it off. She gave it a good looking over.

'Āe, this is what I've been searching for,' she remarked.

Nana placed the cone to her ear, closed her eyes, and listened intently.

Pipi walked over.

'Careful, Nan,' she chuckled. 'There might be a hermit crab living in there. It'll crawl into your ear and make a home in your brain.'

'Eww,' the little kids cringed, feeling their ears to make sure nothing was trying to sneak in.

Nana raised a finger to show that she was busy.

Pipi bent down and met her grandmother's gaze. 'What are you doing?'

'Can't you see?' the tohunga whispered. 'I'm on a call right now.'

The wee moko laughed.

'Here we go,' Pipi sighed, rolling her eyes.

What the rug rats didn't realize was that Nana wasn't playing. She was serious, and Pipi could tell from the expression on her face that the message Nana was getting from the shell wasn't a good one.

Nana lowered the cone and looked left, to the cliff and rocks at the far end of the beach.

'Haere mai, Pipi and Pou,' she beckoned. 'Homai taku kete, pass my basket.'

Pou tutted when he heard his name.

'But, Nana, we just finished saying karakia kai,' he argued. 'There's all this food.'

'When it is time for mahi, then it's time for mahi,' preached Nana, struggling to get to her feet. 'There will still be kai when we get back.'

She smiled and handed the opal top shell back to the boy who had found it. He was suddenly popular among the young children who all crowded around him, each wanting a turn to listen to the shell and discover for themselves what Nana had heard. The boy shook the cone vigorously and peered inside for any sign of a brain-infesting crab.

Toru

Nana told the whānau that she, and her
mokopuna, had something to do at the other
end of the beach and that she would return
soon. The family was resistant to her leaving.
They were enjoying everybody being together,
but they also knew that Nana had her ways.
Aunty Kaia suggested that she at least leave Pipi
and Pou behind. Nana said that she needed the
pair.

Pipi and Pou weren't happy. They wanted

to hang out with their cousins and eat the wonderful kai. Their heads were down and they dragged their feet as they followed Nana over the hot sand.

'Why does it have to be us all the time?' Pou moaned, glancing back at the whānau. 'Why are we always the ones who have to make a difference? Can't someone else save the planet for a change? I'm sick of being a superhero.'

He kicked the sand hard with his foot, hitting a buried rock with his toes.

'Ow!' he cried.

Pipi couldn't help but laugh.

'It's not funny!' growled Pou.

'Don't have a go at me!' Pipi snapped. 'I don't want to be here either!'

Pou eyed his grandmother walking ahead. He

knew that she could hear him, however, she just carried on as though he hadn't said anything. Pou turned to Pipi.

'Who told her that something was wrong this time?' he grumbled. 'Was it the wind, a seagull, or the sandman?' He waved his hands about whimsically in front of him.

'Kāo, it was a shell,' Pipi informed him. 'You know, the cone-shaped ones that amplify the sound of the sea when you hold them to your ear.'

Pou shook his head. 'Why can't we have a normal Nana like everybody else?'

'Shows how much you know,' said Nana, without turning around. 'All grandmothers have magic.'

They came to the rocks and the wave-cut

platform which extended out from the cliff face into the sea, forming a border to the bay, Nana ventured onwards, leading her moko up and onto the rough terrain beyond.

'Ouch, watch out for the baby mussels,' Pou warned, curling his bare feet. 'The shells are pointy.'

'The rocks are sharp too,' Pipi complained. 'If I had known that we were going rock climbing, I would have worn my shoes.'

She paused taking a moment to watch the waves crash against the edges of the outcrop. She tasted the salt air on her lips and could hear the sounds of people having fun back on the beach behind her. A flock of seagulls flew overhead.

'There's a pātangatanga,' announced Pou,

bent over and pointing out a blue cushion starfish in a rock pool.

Pipi joined him in admiring the creature. Her eyes scanned the rest of the pool searching for more forms of life. She noted chiton stuck to the rock, some cat's eye snails, and other shells.

Kneeling, Pou put his hand in the water and gently prodded a brown, red sea anemone. He giggled when it closed around his finger.

'What's the bet that there are crabs in here?' Pipi supposed.

'No doubt,' agreed Pou. 'They're probably hiding under one of the rocks.'

'Or under those ledges,' Pipi indicated at the bottom of the pool. She lowered herself to get a better look. 'There's one. I can see his purple pincers.'

Pou leaned over her trying to see the crab for himself. 'E Pāpaka, haere mai, get in my puku.'

Pipi laughed and looked up. Nana had rounded the cliff and was now back on the sand, walking the shoreline of the next bay.

'We better get a move on,' Pipi urged, heading after her.

'I'll race ya,' Pou challenged.

The pair found that it wasn't easy running on the craggy, coarse surface.

'Ooh, argh, ooh, argh,' they chorused, as they attempted to jump from rock to rock. It was a relief for the soles of their feet when they were back on the soft sand.

'I would have been much faster if I had my sneakers,' claimed Pou.

Feeling as though each foot had been

tenderised, neither of the cousins were interested in continuing their race. Instead, they walked along in the shallows, splashing one another and running from the oncoming waves.

The pair ran from the sea and up onto the beach where Nana was standing.

The tohunga was studying a calm channel in between the waves.

'This is the place,' she proclaimed.

Catching her breath, Pipi looked around.

'It's just a tide rip, Nan,' she explained. 'You see them all the time. We have to stay away from those, remember. It's a current that will drag you out to sea.'

Nana peered back the way that they had come. She could see past the cliff face to the other beach, where the whānau were gathered.

'No one should see us here,' she declared. 'We're too far away.'

'Why, what's going on?' Pipi queried.

'Haere mai, my moko,' Nana encouraged, kicking off her shoes. 'It's time for you to change. There is someone you have to meet.'

Pipi and Pou shared a glance. They couldn't see anybody else in the bay other than a group of tarāpunga. The red-billed seagulls with their snowy white bodies and silvery grey wings, were standing on the sand near the rocks.

Opening her throat, Nana gave an almighty karanga, calling to the moana. She told the sea who she was, and where she had come from. The tohunga gestured at Pipi and Pou, and stated that the giant eagle and the taniwha were her mokopuna, and that as a whānau they had come in peace.

'We are kaitiaki!' sang Nana. 'Guardians and protectors of the natural world!'

Pou raised his brow at Pipi. He was certain that Nana had well and truly lost her mind this time.

Right at that moment an enormous blob of salt water sprung from the sea and landed on Nana and her moko, drenching them. The trio stood dripping wet, gapping at the moana.

Pipi rubbed her face along her forearm.

'What just happened?' she spluttered.

'The sea spat at us!' Pou exclaimed, pointing at the waves.

'Of course, it wouldn't be easy,' Nana huffed to herself. 'What was I thinking?' She used the edge of her top to wipe the water from her glasses.

'It wasn't the moana spitting at us,' she told her moko. 'But somebody in it.'

The two cousins squinted at the ocean.

Standing tall, Pou slapped his thighs and stomped his foot.

'Taniwha, kia kaha!' he roared, pulling a mighty pūkana.

There was a flash of light and Pou turned into a taniwha, a monster.

Pipi closed her eyes and took a deep breath.

Following her cousin, she sprung into the air.

'Pouākai, haere mai!' she roared, pulling a mighty pūkana.

There was another flare of light and Pipi changed into a pouākai, a giant eagle.

Flapping her enormous wings, she flew straight up into the air.

Pou te Taniwha weaved into the shallows, searching for an image to go with the danger that he now felt.

'What exactly are we looking for, Nan?' he asked.

Suddenly something in the foamy waves wrapped around his ankle, gripping him tight.

'Hey!' he cried, trying to see what it was that had a hold of him.

Before Pou te Taniwha could say another word, he was wrenched off his feet and dragged out rapidly through the surf by his leg.

'Pou!' Pipi Pouākai squawked.

She spread her wings wide, swooped low, and went after him.

Pou was tossed high into the air.

'Argh!' he howled, as he hurtled away from the beach.

Nana could only watch as her grandson splashed in the deep beyond the breaking waves, seventy metres from her and the shore.

Whā

In the bay, Nana stood where the waves met the beach, while Pipi Pouākai flew off in pursuit of her cousin, Pou te Taniwha, who was now some distance out behind the breakers. The tohunga's hand went to the moko kauae on her chin, and her fingers ran over the engraved lines as she pondered the situation.

Pipi Pouākai soared over the ocean.

'Pou!' she screeched, scanning the rippled water for any sign of her whanaunga.

The taniwha burst from the surface a little way behind her.

'Whoa, that was awesome!' he cheered.

Pipi Pouākai circled, swooping down closer to him. 'Are you okay?'

'Yeah,' he beamed. 'What threw me?'

'I didn't see,' the eagle answered, hovering above. 'Normally I can spot things from miles away with my super vision, but the sea's not the clearest. It's all churned up. I'll take another look though.'

Flapping her pinions she flew about.

'Pouākai, tiro atu ō whatu!' Pipi cried, and with an eagle eye, she attempted to penetrate the depths of the moana.

It didn't take long for her to spot something large in the water.

'What's that?' she said, flying nearer. 'Kāo!'

Pipi Pouākai spun about, aimed her beak skyward, and beat her wings vigorously trying to get away, but just as she started to rise a giant orange tentacle emerged from the ocean and wound around both of her legs. The eagle hardly had enough time to squawk as, with one fell swoop, she was yanked from the air and taken underwater, leaving only a handful of brown feathers floating in the breeze.

Paddling on the surface, Pou te Taniwha was shocked at what he had just witnessed.

Then with a roar, 'I'm coming, Pipi!' he used his mighty strength to swim after his cousin.

He was moving so fast that he never noticed the tentacles reaching out for him until it was too late. Like the eagle, Pou te Taniwha tried to change direction and escape but he was pulled beneath the waves.

At the water's edge, Nana had been keeping an eye on both Pipi and Pou, but now there wasn't any sign of either of them. It was just the rising and falling of the sea.

'E hika!' she gasped, pushing her glasses up on her nose with her finger. 'This is not the fun day at the beach that I had been hoping for.'

She rummaged through her kete and pulled out a conch shell trumpet which had a short wooden mouthpiece attached. It was called a pūtātara. Nana looked about to make sure no one else was around. She always did this when she was about to do something amazing and didn't want anyone to see it. Apart from the flock of tarāpunga, she was alone in the bay.

Nana took a big breath and blew life into the pūtātara. A deep, haunting sound emerged from the wind instrument and spread, resonating over and into the land and sea.

Three giant tentacles suddenly breached the ocean, appearing from deep water just thirty metres from shore and directly in front of the tohunga. The limbs snaked and swirled together in the air, their ends all entangled with a struggling taniwha, but there was no sign of Pipi.

'Don't worry, Nana!' Pou te Taniwha bellowed. 'I've got him right where I want him!'

As quickly as the tentacles had appeared they dropped and vanished back into the salt water, dragging the taniwha down with them.

Holding the pūtātara in both hands, Nana scoured the sea for any glimpse of Pipi and Pou.

'Moko!' she called. 'Moko!'

Rima

Nana stood motionless in the shallows clutching the pūtātara. A soft breeze skimmed over the surface of the sea and blew against her. With a free hand, she held her hat to her head so as not to lose it to the wind. Wave after wave rolled into shore, lapping at Nana's ankles. She was waiting, hoping anxiously for her grandchildren to reappear from the deep, while at the same time trying to think of a way to help them.

'That's a fancy pūtātara you have there,' said a voice.

Startled, Nana turned to find an old man standing in the sand behind her. It was the elder that she had seen under the pōhutukawa when she first arrived at the beach. She noticed that his eyes were crystal blue, mirroring the ocean, and that the many lines on his brown face mimicked the ripples amongst the waves, making it look as though he had a mataora, a full face moko. He had a coiled, woven harakeke rope draping from one shoulder. She assumed that he was on his way to mend a fishing net.

Nana eyed the wind instrument in her hand.

'Āe,' she muttered, glancing out to the moana. 'I thought it might..., do something.'

Nana had to be careful with what she said. She couldn't give away that the pūtātara had special powers.

'Were you calling someone?' the old man queried, studying the waves.

'Well, if I was, I don't think anyone heard it,' Nana sighed.

The elder couldn't have shown up at a worse time. All Nana wanted to do was save Pipi Pouākai and Pou te Taniwha from the clutches of the giant tentacles, and from the monster that those limbs were attached to.

'I heard it,' said the old man.

Nana turned to him. She couldn't put her finger on it, but there was something strangely familiar about the elder, as though she had met him somewhere before. She looked around the beach. It was still empty of other people and there was no longer any sign of the flock of seagulls. Nana gave the man a smile and a nod, then returned her attention to the sea.

'I'm waiting for my moko,' she stated, trying to hide her concern.

She was hoping that the old guy would take the hint and move on.

'I used to have a pūtātara identical to that one,' he mentioned.

'Aha,' Nana murmured, thinking he was talking nonsense. There was no way that anyone could have had a matching conch trumpet. Every pūtātara made was unique. No two were ever the same.

'Āe; however, a couple of patupaiarehe ran off with it,' he continued. 'Apparently, they gave it to someone.'

Nana gulped. It just so happened that a couple of fairies had gifted the pūtātara to her some years back in a ngahere up north, but how would the old man know that?

She put the instrument away in her kete beside her feet and met his gaze. 'Do I know you?'

The elder took a deep breath of the salty sea air.

'It's a good thing your moko were here,' he said, with his hands on his hips. 'Wheke Ripo, the whirlpooling octopus, was heading straight for those people.'

He gestured at the beach where Nan's whānau and other families were enjoying their day, oblivious to the fact that a giant, eight-legged monster was stalking the water.

'Te wheke?' Nana frowned.

It was now clear to her that this man knew more about the situation than she did, and that he even knew who she was.

He took a simple bone fish hook from a cord around his neck and Nana watched him tie it

46

securely onto the end of the woven harakeke rope.

'Try this,' he urged, passing the fishing tackle to her. 'It's my favourite line.'

Nana didn't know what to say or do. Was the man actually helping or was he expecting her to catch him a feed? She stood staring down at the rope.

'You best be quick, Nan,' he stressed. 'Your moko have been underwater for a while now. The taniwha will be okay, but I worry for the eagle. Not really water breathers those things.'

Without further thought, Nana stepped away from the elder, swung the line over her head a few times, and let it fly. The hook hurtled through the air and plunged into the sea a good distance from the shore.

Holding onto the other end of the flax rope, Nana gave it an almighty tug. The line gave, showing that it was loose beneath the waves.

'Nothing,' Nana clucked.

'Don't let it be the one that got away,' the old man chuckled.

He gently touched the rope with his fingers. 'Give it another pull.'

Nana tugged again. The hook snared and the line tightened.

'I've caught something!' cried the tohunga.

There was an enormous roar as the mantle and head of a giant octopus suddenly breached the surface of the sea in a flurry of water, just twenty metres from Nana. The body of the cephalopod was three times the size of her car.

'Wheke Ripo,' the old man declared under his breath, loud enough for Nana to hear.

The sight of the monstrous creature caused the tohunga to fall back. She landed on her bum in the sand. Wheke Ripo reared and roared out again. The colour of his body turned from green to black and spikes grew, extending outwards all over him. Two horns formed on the top of his head. A pair of his large tentacles slid up, out of the ocean and went to his side, where the end of the hook was protruding from his skin. Nana could see that he was trying to remove the barb with his suckers.

Wheke Ripo was so big and heavy that Nana knew there was no way that she would get him to shore. She was also certain that the harekeke line and the hook weren't going to be able to hold him for much longer. It was only a matter of seconds before the leviathan would break free.

An octopus typically has eight tentacles, but there were only two above the surface. Nana scanned the depths of the water for his other limbs and for any sign of Pipi or Pou. The sea was churned up from Wheke Ripo thrashing about though, so it was hard to see anything. The tohunga dropped her hands out of frustration causing the line to twitch.

'Ow!' trumpeted Wheke Ripo. His voice came from the yellow siphon stemming out from the side of his head. 'Stop that! It hurts!'

He glared at the old woman with one of his enormous eyes.

Nana felt the woven flax rope in her grasp. It appeared that there was more to this hook and line than she first realised. Wheke Ripo should have been able to escape with little effort, yet for some reason, the fishing tackle had rendered the giant octopus powerless. She jerked the rope again.

'Argh!' Wheke Ripo yelled, his body turning white and the spikes and horns disappearing.

He plunged the two tentacles back into the sea and hurriedly swam towards her and the shore, causing the line to slacken. 'Why ... why would you keep pulling it when you know that it hurts me?'

Nana took up the slack in the rope.

Seeing this, the giant octopus raced her, moving swifter through the tide, pushing a surge of water ahead of him. 'You don't have to keep yanking, lady! I'm coming, okay!'

'Where are my moko?' Nana growled.

'They're safe, I haven't hurt them,' stated

Wheke Ripo, wading in the shallows on three of his tentacles with little effort. The colour of his body changed to grey with brown specks, resembling that of the nearby rocks.

He raised four of his limbs out of the moana and up into the air, revealing Pipi Pouākai and Pou te Taniwha. The cousins were busy wrestling two legs each.

'Kia ora, Nana!' shouted Pipi Pouākai. 'It's all good. Calamari here ain't that tough.'

Swinging his tentacles over the beach, Wheke Ripo attempted to shake off the eagle and the taniwha.

'Let go!' he demanded.

Pipi Pouākai and Pou te Taniwha relented their struggle and dropped, falling onto the sand. Both were quick to get up and face the octopus.

'Here, take your mokopuna,' Wheke Ripo pleaded to Nana. Using his limbs, he crawled onto the shore. 'I don't want them. I've been trying to get them off me for ages. They won't leave me alone.'

'You grabbed us first!' Pipi Pouākai was quick to argue with a flap of her wings. 'We were just trying to bring you to our grandmother!'

The eyes of the octopus narrowed to thin horizontal lines.

'You could've asked?' he scowled.

'Great catch, Nan,' sneered Pou te Taniwha, standing next to her and studying the creature. 'Let's take it home. I feel like squid rings for dinner. Stick him in the freezer and we would have enough kai to feed the hapu for a couple of months.'

Wheke Ripo blew a glob of gunk from his siphon which splatted directly in the taniwha's face.

'Eww!' groaned Pou te Taniwha, trying to wipe the gooey, sticky slime off. 'That's the second time I've been hit in the mug today. What was that, snot?'

'Ha ha, that's what I call kanohi ki te kanohi!' laughed Wheke Ripo. 'Face to face! I'm an octopus, not a squid!' His legs unfurled and waved about. 'Don't you two kiddies know the difference?'

'Still tastes nice,' Pipi Pouākai remarked. 'Especially with some soya sauce and a bit of lemon.'

Wheke Ripo blew from his siphon again, this time squirting a jet of black ink at the eagle.

'Ugh, yuck!' she squawked, beating her pinions and jumping back on the beach.

Nana held up the line.

'Ow!' winced Wheke Ripo.

All at once his eyes squinted even thinner, his squishy body compacted, the tentacles curled up and retracted, and his skin turned white.

'What are you crying about?' Pipi Pouākai huffed, trying to shake the ink and seawater from her feathers. 'That hook is so small compared to the size of you. It can't be hurting that much.'

'That's not fair!' grumbled Wheke Ripo, tentatively pointing with the tip of one of his limbs. 'You're using a magic hook and line. If you didn't have that I would have broken free, paralysed you with my beak, and eaten you fellas already.'

The eagle rolled her eyes.

'Whatever,' she scoffed, dismissively.

'Well, take the hook out and I'll show you!' Wheke Ripo challenged, raising and spreading his mantle while standing tall on three of his eight legs. His horns and spikes reappeared as he morphed into black.

'That's enough,' asserted Nana.

'Haha!' the taniwha laughed at the octopus.

'Pou, that's enough, I said!' Nana repeated.

'See, she wasn't just talking to me,' insisted Wheke Ripo, his form dropping down, spreading out, and becoming yellow and smooth. 'So, shame.'

'Fighting never solves anything,' Nana proclaimed, standing her carved walking stick in front of them. 'You know that.'

Ono

The tohunga lifted her head to the midday light from Tamanuiterā and glanced out at the horizon. It was blue on blue with the sky and sea. Hard to tell where one began and the other ended. They seemed to merge into one another. Nana pressed the front of her feet downwards and felt the sand in between her toes.

'Why are you so upset, Wheke Ripo?' she asked.

The two mound eye sockets that protruded

from either side of the giant octopus's head turned in the direction of the neighbouring bay. With his bluey-black pupils narrowed to horizontal slits, he stared at the people in the surf and on the beach. The noise of their boat engines, laughter, and cries carried through the air, competing with the sound of the nearby waves.

'I just want to gobble them up until there are none left,' Wheke Ripo snarled. 'See how they like it.'

His skin became grey and dull, and his body looked to shrink in size. Nana and her moko followed his gaze.

'They take too much,' the octopus continued. 'The people come day and night. They strip the scallops, mussels, crayfish, pāua, kina and ika.

Deplete everything. This coast used to be full of marine life, but now there is little left. The humans don't let new life grow, they don't allow time for the bays to recover and replenish.' While Wheke Ripo spoke, some of his tentacles reached out to the sea, giving the impression that they had a mind of their own. The legs swayed and danced in the shallows, appearing to appreciate the feel of the water. His mantle inhaled, expanding like a balloon, then deflated as he breathed out his siphon. 'There is no conservation. The eco cycle has been damaged. We, the children of Tangaroa, are dying.'

Hearing this, Pipi Pouākai and Pou te Taniwha didn't feel so good about giving the octopus a hard time.

'We weren't really going to eat you,' claimed the taniwha.

'Āe, we were just playing,' the raptor added.

'I like eating seafood too,' Wheke Ripo replied. 'But I only catch enough kaimoana, never more than I need. The people have taken too much! I am kaitiaki, I have to protect what is left!' Each one of his pupils went from being a line to the shape of a W. His colour turned black and red.

The whānau observed two horns forming on top of his head, along with spikes that began to jut out all over his body, just as they had done earlier.

Nana could sense his anger.

'Āe, Wheke Ripo, kei te tika, you are right,' she sympathised.

She approached him, her hand slowly going for the magic hook sticking out from his side.

He flinched, changed white, and moved back from her.

'It hurts,' he said.

'I know,' Nana nodded. 'And the last thing that my moko and I want to do is cause you pain, e te rangatira. Let me remove the hook.'

She slowly extended her hand to him.

Wheke Ripo pulled away. Using the twin line of suckers that ran the length of all eight legs, he pulled in shells and stones from the beach. He wrapped his tentacles over and around his body, displaying the objects outwards. Then through colour, texture, and pattern, the cephalopod transformed himself into a rock.

'Whoa, check out the camouflage!' Pou te Taniwha exclaimed. 'You can't even see him now. Anyone could walk right past Wheke Ripo on the beach and never know that he was an octopus. That's amazing!'

Nana looked through Wheke Ripo's disguise to the barely visible dash that his eye had become.

'Please,' she implored, refusing to let the hook go unattended.

The giant octopus watched her for a moment, then uncoiled and lightened his appearance. Leaning forward he allowed the tohunga to gently remove the barb. The remaining wound was small. Nana blew on it softly, comforting Wheke Ripo. She then took some of her special homemade rongoā from her kete and applied it to the side of the octopus.

'This will help to heal the injury,' she explained.

Wheke Ripo waved his tentacles about, shook his body, and became yellow.

'I can't feel anything now,' he noted, amazed. 'Auē, it was the magic of the hook and line that made it painful.' His eyes opened wider and he peered at the barb in Nana's hand while she wound the flax woven rope. 'Such a little thing can cause so much trouble.'

'A bit like a ngaro huruhuru,' Pipi Pouākai commented. 'Our taniwha here flinches whenever one of them shows up.'

'That was one time!' Pou te Taniwha protested. 'And that wasn't a normal native bee. Its sting hurt.'

'I once lost a tentacle to a monster of a shark called Kaitohorā, Whale Eater,' Wheke Ripo told the whānau. 'That mangō taniwha grabbed hold with his jaws and spun about in a death roll until it ripped off. There was so much of my blue blood spilling that it was hard to see, and that wasn't anywhere as sore as that hook was.'

The eagle and the taniwha proceeded to count his tentacles.

'My legs grow back,' he informed them, holding up two.

'Wicked,' uttered the taniwha. 'I wish mine could do that.'

Pipi Pouākai took a step back to take in the size of the giant Wheke Ripo. She then gazed out at the sea with concern. 'That must have been one massive as shark.'

Jiggling like jelly, Wheke Ripo turned about in a circle. 'I don't feel anything now. No pain at all.'

'Hei aha, be that as it may, aroha mai,' Nana reiterated, placing the hook and line down on the sand. 'We are sorry for the way that we treated you.'

Pink appeared in Wheke Ripo's face. His eyes became big and round.

'It's not like I behaved any better,' he sighed. He glanced at Pipi Pouākai and Pou te Taniwha. 'I did drag your grandchildren underwater.'

Grasping the top of her tokotoko with both hands, Nana smiled. 'I must admit, I was worried. I'm happy that you returned them unharmed, though.'

'We were fine,' said Pipi Pouākai, not wanting her grandmother to overreact.

'It was awesome!' Pou te Taniwha stressed. 'I haven't had a good wrestle like that in ages.'

Nana gave the hook mark on the side of the octopus one more rub. 'This is one pain attended to. Now we must address the mamae of the bay.' Her eyes met those of Wheke Ripo. 'E te rangatira, I don't think that eating the people is going to help. Lashing out in anger only brings hurt and trouble. I'm just happy that this old man turned up to help when he did.' Nana gestured over her shoulder at the beach behind her. 'Otherwise, the crowds over there would have noticed, and you are someone that they would hunt down, Wheke Ripo. I've never known an octopus that has lived as long as you. You're a taonga, a treasure, that they would pursue.'

Pipi Pouākai, Pou te Taniwha, and Wheke Ripo shared a look.

'Old man?' the eagle questioned, examining their surroundings. 'Who are you talking about, Nan?'

The tohunga pushed the glasses up on her nose and turned about. The flock of tarāpunga were back, standing guard on the sand, however, the elder who had given Nana the magic line and hook was nowhere to be seen.

'Where did that old fella go?' she wondered aloud, her eyes scanning the foreshore.

'Are you okay, Nan?' Pipi Pouākai queried further. 'Perhaps you've had too much sun for one day.'

'You probably need a lie-down and a cup of tea?' suggested Pou te Taniwha. 'Your blood sugar levels might be low.'

'Hmm,' Nana murmured, her fingers from one hand exploring the moko kauae on her chin. She studied the gulls. 'Isn't that interesting.'

Whitu

Wheke Ripo extended a tentacle out to Nana.
The tohunga allowed the limb to feel its
way over her forearm with its white suckers.
Through the touch, Nana sensed a deep
connection with the animal. The tentacle
wrapped around her arm and the suckers
clutched on firmly.

'I heard your karanga on the beach,' said
Wheke Ripo.

Nana felt his words vibrate up her arm and
through her body.

'You said that you were kaitiaki,' the octopus went on. 'Guardians and protectors of the natural world.'

'Āe, I also said that we came in peace,' Nana's eyes twinkled. 'But that was before you and my moko ended up having a tussle in the sea.'

Wheke Ripo reached out to Pipi Pouākai and Pou te Taniwha. Following their grandmother's example, the eagle put out a wing, the taniwha an arm, and each locked their limb with the octopus.

'Will you awhi and tautoko me and my bays?' Wheke Ripo questioned.

Pou te Taniwha glanced at his cousin.

'Whoa, I can feel his voice inside me,' he grinned. 'The words of the octopus are echoing through my body. Can you feel it, too?'

Pipi Pouākai chirped. 'It's like it's just him, us, the waves, and nothing else.'

Nana looked at Wheke Ripo with a serious expression.

'E te rangatira, ngā mihi nui ki a koe,' she offered. 'I acknowledge you, chief. Thank you for letting me and my mokopuna into your world. I will do all that I can to ensure that this coastline gets the rest it needs to replenish, and the ongoing protection it requires so that it may thrive in the future.'

Wheke Ripo closed his eyes and bowed his head to Nana, showing respect and gratitude.

Pipi Pouākai fluffed her feathers.

'Huri hei kōtiro!' she cried, turning into a girl.

Her cousin copied her.

'Huri hei tama!' Pou te taniwha roared, becoming a boy.

The octopus was delighted by the changes.

'Wow, shape-shifters,' he remarked. 'You were an eagle, and you were a monster, but now you are both people. That's so cool. I can alter my appearance as well.'

'Are you kidding me?' Pipi blurted. 'Seriously?'

Wheke Ripo turned to Nana. 'He aha, did I say something wrong?'

'E te rangatira,' Pipi addressed the giant octopus. 'You are the master of transformation. You are like a rainbow. I've lost count of the number of colours that I've seen you become today. And as for shape-shifting, one minute you're enormous and towering over us, the next you're squeezing into tiny gaps in the rocks, or flat like a pancake, and then you are camouflaged and blending into your surroundings.'

'Breathe girl,' Nana pressed, concerned that Pipi wasn't getting enough oxygen with all her ranting.

Pipi held up a hand to show that she hadn't finished saying what she had to say. 'You can appear bumpy, smooth, or spikey with horns, Wheke Ripo. During our wrestle in the moana, I couldn't keep track of you, and the different forms that you took.'

'True,' nodded Pou. 'More powerful than any superhero I know. Like something out of a movie. I never knew an octopus could do all that.'

Wheke Ripo was speechless, yet the shade of yellow he became was bright and loud. The colour of pāua shell circled his eyes.

'I would give anything to have half the abilities that you have,' declared Pipi. 'For real, you are the coolest. And how many hearts do you have? Three isn't it?'

'Āe,' Nana affirmed.

'That just shows the amount of aroha that you deserve,' Pipi pronounced. 'Enough love for three hearts.'

A sparkle appeared in the now round eyes of the octopus. He uncoiled his tentacles from the arms of each whanau member.

'It seems to me that your ability to care and love is your greatest power, Ms Pouākai,' he said. 'Such power can transform the world. I thank you for your kind words, and for your help and support.'

'Don't thank us,' Pipi uttered. 'What's happening to these bays is not okay. It should never have come to this. People need to be careful and gentle with our world. If it wasn't for you grabbing us, then we would never have known how bad it had gotten around here. So, it is us who are indebted to you.'

'Kia ora, Pipi,' Pou grinned.

She glared at her cousin.

'I'm being serious,' she retorted, flicking sand at him with her foot.

'So am I,' Pou chuckled. 'I agree with what you said. I just haven't seen you on a soap box before, you little speechmaker, you.'

Nana proudly patted the girl on the back.

Wheke Ripo peered past the cliff face to the next bay where the whānau and other people continued to enjoy their day in the sun.

'I spent all morning working myself up to attack the beach and eat that lot,' he groaned.

'I was so nervous.' The loose skin around the base of his body spread out like a web. His tentacles explored the sand and shallows about them, and his colour changed again, mimicking the backdrop. 'I'm pretty sure I would have gotten a stomach ache from gobbling them though.'

Nana placed a hand on the side of his mantle. 'It's best you stay hidden, Wheke Ripo. If someone caught sight of you, the glory hunters would want to catch you. I hate to say it, but you would make a fine trophy for any museum or fishing show.'

The octopus flexed his limbs. 'I reckon I could take them.'

Nana peered over the top of her glasses.

'We're here,' she stated, gesturing at her moko. 'Let us fight this battle for you instead.'

Wheke Ripo raised three of his tentacles in the air and looked them over.

'If I'm not going to attack, then what do I do with all this built-up energy?'

Pou raised his hand.

'I've been thinking about that,' he said.

Nana, Pipi, and Wheke Ripo faced him.

'E te rangatira,' he uttered with reverence. 'Can you throw me again?'

Frown lines appeared on Nana's face.

'Excuse me?' she muttered, pursing her lips.

'It was sick!' Pou emphasized, before going into a dramatic, physical performance of the whole experience right there on the sand. 'I was grabbed in the water. I was like, *what*? Then I was flying through the air, like argh! Then sploshed in the sea, like wahoo! It was better than any ride I've ever been on. I'm telling ya, you could sell tickets. People would be lining up to have a go.'

Pipi smiled. 'It did look fun.'

'I'm sure Wheke Ripo has far more important things to do than to be tossing you two about,' Nana rebuked.

'C'mon, Nan,' pleaded Pou. 'We came to the beach to have a good time and enjoy the water. I'm sure Wheke Ripo won't mind.'

He turned to the giant.

The octopus scratched the top of his mantle with the end of a tentacle.

'Are you two really sure that you can handle the might that is Wheke Ripo?' he challenged, playfully.

'Bring it,' giggled Pipi.

'Lit!' Pou cried, with a fist pump. 'Hey, what?'

He glanced down to see that while one tentacle was scratching the crown of Wheke Ripo, another had sneakily wrapped around his ankle.

'Mā te wā, e taniwha,' rhymed Wheke Ripo. 'See you later.'

'Ahh!' Pou yelled as the tentacle fired him like a slingshot, flinging him into the air and out over the sea.

Nana and Pipi watched him go.

'E hika, look at that boy fly!' the tohunga exclaimed.

She saw him splash into deep water a short distance from the shore. He was quick to re-emerge to the surface, cheering and waving both fists over his head triumphantly.

'He's fine,' Nana mumbled, reassuring herself.

A tentacle coiled around Pipi's waist.

'Are you ready to fly, Ms Pouākai?' the octopus queried.

She nodded.

Wheke Ripo threw her out over the moana.

'Weeee!' Pipi cried. 'I'm flying without wings!'

Nana and Wheke Ripo both laughed when the girl plopped into the sea.

Two tentacles reached out to the tohunga.

Nana stepped back and pointed at the octopus with her tokotoko.

'Don't you dare!' she snapped, looking most indignant. 'You're not throwing me like that.'

'Suit yourself,' Wheke Ripo cackled.

His legs carried him into the water and from there he swam out to meet Pipi and Pou.

Nana took a deep breath, leaned on her walking stick, and smiled, while she watched

her moko play in the ocean with the leviathan,
Wheke Ripo.

Waru

The sun glistened over the surface of the sea as wave after wave followed one another and washed into shore. Nana could hear the cries of joy from her grandchildren as they enjoyed their time with Wheke Ripo.

'Nana, watch this!' Pipi yelled from the water.

Wheke Ripo threw her with one of his tentacles. The girl flew over the head of the octopus where he caught her with another of his limbs and dunked her beneath the surface. After a couple of seconds, Pipi resurfaced back where she had first begun, having completed a full circle.

'Do me, do me!' Pou begged, paddling towards them.

Wheke Ripo took hold of both of the cousins and proceeded to cycle them through his tentacles, over from left to right in the air, and then under the water back to the left. Around and around, they went like riding a Ferris wheel.

Nana chuckled and waved to the kids.

She looked back to the beach where her whānau had set up camp for the day. The tohunga was amazed that no one had noticed the octopus throwing her moko around or come to find out what they were doing. Especially when Pipi and Pou were making so much noise.

Nana became aware that someone was standing beside her.

'You were a young fella the last time I saw you,' she said, turning to the old man. 'That was only two years ago. So, it is no wonder I didn't recognise you under the pōhutukawa this morning.'

The elder watched Pipi and Pou frolic in the surf with the giant octopus.

'The flock of tarāpunga was a good trick,' Nana continued. 'I'm more used to your brother, Tāne-mahuta, the father of the forest, being the shapeshifter in your family.'

He shrugged. 'Young, old, human, whale, red-billed gulls, I take whatever form works.'

The tohunga bowed her head. 'It's nice to know that Wheke Ripo has the backing of

Tangaroa, the matua of the sea. E te rangatira, tēnā koe.'

'Tēnā koe, Nan,' Tangaroa answered. 'I'm just glad that you're here. That you were able to settle Wheke Ripo.' He took a deep breath. 'I have tried to kōrero with the hau kāinga. Suggested to the local people that they place a rāhui on the bay, to ban the collecting of kaimoana, and allow time for the coastline to heal and recover. Even went as far as recommending that they turn a part of the coast into a marine reserve to preserve it for the future.' Tangaroa shook his head. 'I may be the atua of the sea, but to them, I was some crazy old, homeless guy. No one recognised me, and they wouldn't listen.' He met her gaze. 'What will it take for them to hear? A tsunami? I can arrange one.'

'I will speak with the people,' said Nana. 'Echo your words.'

'Ngā mihi nui ki a koe, Nan,' the elder replied. 'I'm sure that they will listen to you and your renowned mana.'

'Well, it is easy to ignore one voice, but harder when there are more,' she offered.

Reaching down, Nana took the magic harakeke line and bone hook and handed them to Tangaroa.

'I suppose you want your pūtātara too,' she muttered as she searched her kete.

Tangaroa chuckled. 'Kāo, you hold onto it for now. Those patupaiarehe obviously thought that you were the right person to have it, and considering the important work that you and your amazing mokopuna are doing, I would

agree.' He put his arm through the harakeke line and draped it over his shoulder. 'Oh, and when you see those cheeky fairies again, tell them that I am looking for them.'

Nana laughed. 'I will, matua.'

'Mā te wā,' he smiled.

The tohunga bowed slightly. 'Āe, mā te wā.'

She watched the old man walk off down the beach.

Iwa

The whānau spent most of the day with Wheke Ripo. They talked and played games like hide and seek, which wasn't fair as the giant octopus was too good at changing his appearance and blending into his surroundings. Wheke Ripo even took Pipi and Pou underwater, through a forest of tall, lush green kelp to show them his den, which was in an enormous crevice on the ocean floor.

After lots of hugs and promises to come

back to visit him, Nana and her moko finally said goodbye to the octopus. Wheke Ripo submerged, descending into the moana, and Nana, Pipi and Pou headed back towards the neighbouring bay. At the beginning of their adventure, the grandchildren had trailed behind their grandmother, refusing to walk with her. Now they marched alongside.

'That was the coolest,' Pipi beamed.

Nana glanced at her.

'Really?' she queried. 'So leaving the family picnic to awhi and tautoko the natural world wasn't such a bore after all, nē?'

Pipi screwed up her face.

'Well, I mean, I would've liked to have spent the day with the whānau too, playing with the cousins and that, so I wasn't happy when we left, but Wheke Ripo was awesome. I had such a good time with him.'

Together they stepped up onto the rocks to cross the wave-cut platform in front of the cliff face. Spray from the waves hitting the edge of the shelf splatted over nearby stones, almost wetting the trio.

'Our adventures with you are always amazing, Nan,' Pou piped up. He was looking for smooth surfaces for his feet as he jumped along the rough terrain. 'I know I'm not always keen in the beginning, but once we get there it's always fun.'

Pipi paused, studying Nana. 'We saw you on the beach with an old man. Was he the one who gave you the magical line and hook?'

'Āe, you'll meet him one day,' the tohunga nodded at the sea.

They walked the sand, weaving their way through people sitting in groups, children running to and from the shallows, and freshly made miniature castles.

'Don't kick those, cousin,' Pipi teased, pointing at the sculptures and reminding Pou of when he had hit a rock with his toes earlier in the day.

'Ha, ha, very funny ... not,' he retorted.

Aunty Kaia smiled from the mat when Nana and the two moko appeared.

'So much for being back soon, Nan,' she commented. She gestured at the other adults sitting around her. 'We were starting to think that we should send a search party out for you three.'

'Āe, we got caught up,' responded Nana,

walking over to the whānau and leaning on her tokotoko. 'I was talking to some old guy who's concerned about the area.'

Aunty Kaia looked worried. 'Really? Why, what's wrong?'

The family made room and beckoned Nana to sit. The tohunga took up the offer, planting herself down with a grunt and a groan. She then proceeded to tell Aunty Kaia and the others about the state of the bays, how the kaimoana had been depleted, and how a rāhui on the coastline was required.

Pipi and Pou were approached by their cousins.

'Where have you guys been?' queried Rāwiri, Aunty Kaia's son.

'At the next beach,' Pipi answered, looking

back and indicating where they had come from. 'It was rad.'

Their young relatives were intrigued.

'Why, what were you doing?' Rāwiri asked further.

Pipi and Pou shared a glance. They couldn't tell anyone about Wheke Ripo. Nobody could find out that a giant octopus was living nearby, otherwise people would go looking for him.

'We had a swim,' said Pou.

'Is that it?' Rāwiri wasn't impressed. 'Just the two of you? What's fun about swimming by yourselves?' He glanced around at the other kids. 'At least we were all together and had the surfboards and that.'

Aunty Kaia got to her feet and started to organise everyone to pack up for home time.

Pou's shoulders dropped.

'Where's all the kai,' he moaned quietly to Pipi. 'I'm starving.'

'It must have gone,' she murmured, feeling her puku rumble.

While Pipi and Pou helped their cousins put things away in the cars, Nana and other adults went and spoke to the hau kāinga at the nearest marae. They sat with three local elders outside the wharekai drinking cups of tea and admiring the view of a mountain and a river.

'You're not the first to come and kōrero to us about the state of our moana,' a kaumātua told them. 'An old fella turned up and shared his concern a while back.'

'Is that right?' Nana frowned, trying to look surprised. She knew it must have been Tangaroa.

A kuia sighed. 'Others didn't want to listen. Told the man to go away. They want to be able to keep fishing here, even though there is less and less to catch.'

Nana closed her eyes and took a deep breath. Those people had no idea that they had rejected the father of the sea.

'Every bit of feedback helps,' the kaumātua continued. 'Some of us have been pushing for a rāhui for a while, to ban the collecting of kaimoana. And now, with enough voices, we can proceed. Especially with you and your whānau involved, Nan.'

As Tangaroa had predicted, Nana's reputation and mana meant that people would hear and take her seriously. The tohunga was known for her mahi across the motu.

'I also hope that a marine reserve for a part of the coastline can be considered,' Nana suggested. 'To prevent the depletion from happening again.'

'Āe, mana whenua, mana moana, mana tangata,' the kaumātua stated. We are the land and the sea, and they are us. We will discuss the prospect of a marine reserve within our hapū. In the meantime, the rāhui will take effect immediately. We will erect a pou, a pillar, to signify the ban. Our coastline will replenish.'

'Kia ora,' Nana uttered, reiterating her support. 'We are kaitiaki. It is what we do.'

The elders nodded in agreement.

When Nana returned to the bay everything belonging to the whānau had been packed and put away. Aunty Kaia and the other whanaunga were sitting on the grass singing waiata with Uncle Hēmi strumming his guitar, and tamariki were playing in the sand. Tamanuiterā was setting and the beach was quieter and calmer now. Nana stood for a moment beneath the bright red and green pōhutukawa where she had first seen Tangaroa. She peered out over the moana. A breeze toyed with her grey hair as she listened to the waves rolling into shore, and thought of a giant octopus.

'There you go, Wheke Ripo,' she softly murmured. 'Your waters will get the rest they need.'

Noticing Nana's return, Aunty Kaia got up from the ground. 'Haere tonu whānau! Let's keep moving. Time to hit the road!'

Nana and the other adults went around, giving each member of the family a hongi, a kiss on the cheek, and a hug. Pipi and Pou did the same. Then they climbed into Nana's old car.

The tohunga inserted the key in the ignition.

'Betsy isn't going to start without a song,' she said. 'You know how sentimental this waka is.'

'It's Pou's turn,' Pipi announced from beside her in the front. She glanced over her shoulder to the back. 'I did it last.'

'What?' Pou tutted, slumping in his seat. 'I can't sing, I still haven't had anything to eat.'

There was a tap on Nana's window. It was Aunty Kaia holding a bowl.

Nana opened her door.

'You can't go home empty-handed, Nan,' beamed Aunty Kaia. 'The three of you must be starving since you missed out on lunch. There was heaps of kai left over, so you take some home.'

The jaws of Pipi and Pou both dropped. The kids couldn't believe their luck. They sat up, excited to see what delights awaited them, but as usual, Nana refused to accept the gift.

'Kāo, you keep it for you and your family, girl,' she urged.

Thankfully Aunty Kaia wasn't taking no for an answer. Instead, she and Rāwiri rushed about, taking plates, bowls, and pots from their car and loading them into Nana's. In no time Pipi and Pou were surrounded by kai.

'Auē,' Nana sighed. 'It's too much.'

'It's no good for me,' Aunty Kaia remarked, rubbing her puku with her hand. 'I'm trying to lose weight,' she chuckled.

'Yeah, but?' Nana tried to argue.

'Whānau hard, Nan,' Aunty Kaia said. 'Love youse.'

She gave Nana one last peck on the side of her face, closed the door, and retreated with Rāwiri back to their vehicle.

Nana eyed the grins on the faces of her two moko.

'I can sing now,' Pou sang, holding up a buttered piece of Rēwena bread dipped in mussel chowder.

Nana turned the key and Betsy sprung to life.

103

104

Glossary

āe – Yes

Aotearoa – Māori name for New Zealand

aroha – love

aroha mai – sorry

ātaahua – beautiful

atua – god

auē – heck, oh dear

awhi – to embrace

āwhina – assistance/support

e – a term of address

e hika! – good heavens! Far out!

haere mai – come, welcome

haere tonu – keep going

hapū – subtribe

harakeke – a flax plant endemic to Aotearoa

hau kāinga – local home people of a marae/home people

he aha – what?

hei aha – expression meaning, be that as it may

homai taku kete – pass my basket

hongi – to press noses in greeting

hui – gathering/meeting

Huri hei kōtiro – the command Pipi uses to transform from an eagle into a girl.

Huri hei tama – the command Pou uses to transform from a taniwha into a boy.

Ika – fish

iwa – nine

kai – food

kaitiaki – guardian/custodian

kaimoana – seafood

kanohi ki te kanohi – face to face

kāo – no

karanga – formal call

karakia kai – giving thanks for food

karakia mō te kai – giving thanks for the food

kaumātua – elderly man/men

kei te pai – fine/good

kei te pēhea koe – how are you?

kete – basket

kia kaha – be strong, keep going

kia ora – hello/cheers

kina – common sea urchin

kōrero – speak/talk

kuia – elderly woman/women

mā te wā – see you later

mahi – work

mamae – hurt

mana – prestige

mana moana – authority over the sea

mana tangata – prestige of the people

mana whenua – power from the land

mangō taniwha – monster shark

marae – courtyard in front of the wharenui, and the group of buildings around it.

matangongore – opal top shell endemic to Aotearoa

mataora – traditional male full–face tattoo

mātua – father

moana – sea

moko – Māori tattooing design

moko – grandchild/grandchildren

mokopuna – grandchild/grandchildren

moko kauae – traditional female chin tattoo

motu – country/land

nē – is that so?

ngā mihi nui – thank you

ngā mihi nui ki a koe – an expression used to acknowledge someone

ngahere – forest

ngaro huruhuru – a bee species native to Aotearoa

ono – six

pāpaka – crab

pātangatanga – star fish

patupaiarehe – fairy folk

pāua – species of large edible sea snails native to Aotearoa

pōhutukawa – a coastal evergreen tree endemic to Aotearoa

pou – pillar

pouākai – an extinct species of giant eagle from Aotearoa

Pouākai, haere mai – the command Pipi uses to transform into an eagle

pouākai, tiro atu ō whatu – the command Pipi says to use her eagle eye vision

Pouākai, titiro mai! – the command Pipi uses for her super eagle vision

pūkana – to stare wildly, dilate the eyes

puku – stomach

pūtātara – conch shell trumpet

rāhui – embargo, traditional ban

rangatira – chief, noble, esteemed, revered

rēwena – bread made with potato yeast

rima – five

rongoā – traditional medicine

rua – two

tahi – one

Tamanuiterā – personification and sacred name of the sun

tamariki – children

Tāne-mahuta – father/god of the forest and birds

Tangaroa – father/god of the sea

taniwha – monster

taniwha kia kaha! – the command Pou uses to transform from a boy into a taniwha.

taonga – treasure

tarāpunga – red-billed gull native to Aotearoa

tautoko – to support

te – the

tēnā koe – hello to one and a way to say thank you.

tēnā koutou – hello to three or more

tika – correct, right

titiro – look

tohunga – expert

tokotoko – carved walking stick

toru – three

waiata – song/sing

waka – vehicle

waru – eight

whā – four

whānau – family

whanaunga – relative/relatives

wharekai – dining hall

wheke – octopus

whitu – seven

Character's names

Kaitohorā – Character name meaning eater of whales.

Wheke Ripo – whirlpooling octopus

If you enjoyed this adventure with Pipi and Pou and their Nan, then try reading another story in the series.

Pipi and Pou and the River Monster

9781990035234

Something fierce and dangerous is hidden around this river and our heros must find it. But maybe social media is the answer. You can read the first chapter here . . .

pipiandpou.com

The first chapter of Pipi and Pou and the River Monster

Tahi

Nana was on her knees weeding in the garden when she heard Kāhu calling from high in the sky. The tohunga sat back on the green grass looking up at the harrier hawk, and listened. A breeze blew through her grey hair and the morning glare from Tamanuiterā, the sun, made her moko kauae shine. Whero, the ginger cat, peered out at her from his hiding spot within the overgrown weeds.

'Haere mai, my moko!' cried Nana, using her

tokotoko to help her get up from the ground. 'We're hitting the road!'

When Nana called out like that, Pipi and Pou knew that it was time to listen. The two cousins closed their books and raced outside to the backyard.

'What's happening, Nan?' asked Pipi.

Nana was brushing bits of grass from her pants. 'We've got to go up north,' she said. 'Something's not right.'

Pipi looked around.

'Was the wind talking to you again?' She remembered the last time Nana had whisked them off on an adventure because the breeze had told her that there was trouble down south.

'Don't be silly,' muttered Nana. 'It was Kāhu.'

Puzzled, Pou turned to his cousin. 'Kāhu?'

The first chapter of Pipi and Pou and the River Monster

Pipi didn't know who Nana was talking about either. The only person that she knew called Kāhu was a five year old at kura.

'Did they phone you?' she asked.

Nana looked at the girl as though she was being absurd. 'Why would Kāhu use a phone? He's right here.' She pointed up.

Pipi and Pou saw the hawk with his wings outstretched, circling high above.

'Ohhh, that Kāhu,' Pipi intoned.

Her grandmother had always believed that she could talk to birds.

'Who else?' Nana frowned.

The two cousins were quiet, watching the raptor.

'Some people might say you're weird, Nan,' Pipi commented.

'There is no other way to be, girl,' she replied.

'So something's not right up north?' Pou asked. 'What is it exactly?'

He was thinking that the reason for this trip was too vague. Pou wanted more information before he was willing to leave home.

His grandmother shrugged. 'I guess we'll find out when we get there.'

Spotting the large, green eyes of Whero peeking out from the garden, Nana poked at the weeds playfully with her tokotoko. A ginger paw swiped at the carved walking stick.

Pipi laughed at the cute cat.

'I'll leave the rest of the mahi to you, puss,' Nana chuckled.

She looked her moko up and down.

The first chapter of Pipi and Pou and the River Monster

'What you're wearing is okay,' she noted. 'Just grab a jacket and your shoes. I'm going to need my kete, and we better take some kai too.'

The old woman headed for the whare.

'How long is this going to take?' Pou quizzed.

Nana faced him. 'Why? Have you got some place that you need to be?'

'No,' he mumbled. 'It's just that it's Sunday and I've nearly finished my book.'

'I'm almost at the end of mine, too,' Pipi echoed. 'It's the third book from the zombie series that I've been reading.'

Nana was never one to get in the way of a good story.

'Bring your pukapuka with you,' she encouraged. 'You can read them on the drive.'

'I feel sick when I read in the car,' argued Pou.

Nana paused, resting both hands atop her tokotoko. She peered over her glasses at her moko.

'What are we?' she gently asked.

'Kaitiaki,' answered Pipi.

'Guardians and protectors of the natural world,' Pou droned.

One thing about living with Nana was that it was never boring. Most weekends she had Pipi and Pou travelling the motu on some mission to protect and save the environment. It wasn't that the kids didn't enjoy the adventures. They loved being superheroes. It was just that sometimes they wanted to relax, to be lazy, to read a book, play on screens, watch television. There was nothing like being still after a long week at school.

The first chapter of Pipi and Pou and the River Monster

Nana lifted her gaze skyward.

'I guess I'll have to tell Kāhu that we can't help him this time,' she muttered.

Pipi and Pou heard the hawk cry out from above. Suddenly their books didn't seem as important.

'It's all right, we can finish our novels when we get back,' Pipi smiled.

'Yeah, I should probably have a break anyway,' agreed Pou. 'I read a lot yesterday.'

Nana pushed her glasses up on her nose with her forefinger. She eyed her grandchildren with pride.

'Right then,' she choked. 'Let's grab our things, and hit the road.'

A short time later Nana and her moko hopped into her old car, Betsy.

'Man, it's always messy in here,' Pou grumbled, pushing clothes and chip packets aside so that he could sit in the back.

'Tēnā koe, boy,' Nana beamed. 'Thank you for offering to clean my waka.'

Pou's eyes narrowed. 'Eh?'

'Shame,' Pipi sniggered, looking back at her cousin from the front passenger seat.

'Don't worry, Pou,' Nana went on. 'Your cousin will be helping you.'

'Uh what?' grumbled Pipi.

It was Pou's turn to laugh.

'None of those things in the back belong to me,' Nana declared. 'I didn't leave them there. How many times have I told you two to put your stuff away?'

Pipi and Pou sat quiet. Having their

The first chapter of Pipi and Pou and the River Monster

grandmother tell them to sort out their belongings was nothing new. They had heard it many times before.

Nana turned the key in the car's ignition, but the engine didn't start.

The tohunga looked at Pipi.

'Betsy's run out of love,' she murmured.

Taking a deep breath, Pipi began to sing a waiata. It was one of her favourites.

Nana tried the key again and the car sprang to life with a cough and a splutter.

She winked at Pipi.

'The old girl loves your singing,' Nana chuckled, patting the dashboard. 'Aroha and waiata, that's what this waka runs on.'

Leaving their driveway, Nana and her moko slowly chugged off down the road.